Dax and the Destroyers

House Flip

Book 1

By: Marcy Blesy

Introduction:

It all started with *Evie and the Volunteers,* a group of girls who spend their time volunteering around town. Though their intentions are always good, they can't seem to stay out of trouble. Check out their stories in books 1-5, *Evie and the Volunteers: Animal Shelter, Nursing Home, After-School Program, Food Pantry, and Public Library.* In this new series, *Dax and the Destroyers,* Dax, a new friend/annoying adversary of Evie, finds his own project. And, like with Evie, trouble is never far away.

Chapter 1:

"Dax Butterfield Johnson!"

There's something about hearing your entire name spoken aloud by your parent that makes your hair stand up on your arms, especially when you've been cursed with a middle name like *Butterfield*, a nod to my mother's unmarried name. I consider pulling the covers back over my head and pretending I didn't hear her, but I know my mom. She won't stop until I acknowledge that I'm alive. I kick off the covers, roll out of bed, pull on the nearest pair of pants I can find which happens to be a wrinkled pair of khakis I wore to church last Sunday that never made it to my closet, and stomp down the stairs—for effect. "Good morning to you, too, Mom," I say, plastering a fake smile on my face.

"Dax, I told you to be ready by 7:15 if you want a ride to school. I have a big presentation at work today. I can't be late."

"Relax, Mom. You've got this." I kiss her on the cheek. That always softens her up.

She sighs. "You're going to wear those pants to school?" She wrinkles her brow.

"If they're good enough for church, I think they're good enough for school, don't you?" I raise one eyebrow at her like I do when I try to get my science teacher Mrs. Carmichael to go easy on me with her punishments. Like it's my responsibility to make sure all the chemicals in the classroom storage closet are safely locked away. Some unknowing boy like myself could get hurt mixing the wrong chemicals. And it wasn't a big fire. That's why there's a fire extinguisher in the classroom, after all. The eyebrow works on mom, too.

"Fine, grab a breakfast bar, run a comb through that hair, grab your backpack, and meet me in the car." She's in the garage before I can say anything more.

It's not that I don't like school. School can be cool. I have my friends. I have teachers to torment—like Mrs. Carmichael. I even like to learn a little stuff, but I'd never admit it. I don't like having to follow someone else's schedule. I like to be the boss of my time. That's why I like the idea that in one more week I'll be free. School will be over for the year, and since Mom is so busy at work, and Dad's gone all the time flying around the world as a commercial jet pilot, I've been given permission to spend the summer with Grandma Julie in Bridgport. Plus, ever since Grandma's car accident over winter break, she's a little slower than she used to be. Mom liked the idea of me spending time with Grandma when I asked if I could spend summer there. It was the easiest argument I never had to make. Plus, it will give me a chance to bug Evie and her volunteer friends. They're cool, but it's so fun getting under their skin. They will give me some much needed entertainment when I'm bored. Who knows, maybe I'll form my own volunteer group—Dax and the Defenders—*Defending our right to do things our way.* Yeah, I totally need that on a shirt.

Chapter 2:

"Listen to your Grandmother. She's the boss. Do things for her, just because, not just when she asks you to. And no stunts. She doesn't need to deal with that. And I certainly don't want to be called out of work to drive two hours to tend to your troubles. Do you understand, *young man?*"

"Mom, relax. When have I ever gotten into trouble?" I know my grin looks goofy because I can feel it lopsided on my face, but that's just me.

"Sarah, Dax will be fine. He's a good boy," says Grandma.

"Aww, thanks, Grandma. You're the best."

Mom sighs for about the tenth time this morning. "Okay, you two behave together then. I'll call every night. Let me know if you need anything, *anytime*, okay?" She hugs her mom.

"I will, Sarah. Travel safely."

We watch Mom back out of the driveway. She's not even at the first stop sign at the end of the road before Grandma spills the biggest secret I've ever heard.

"Your mother was a tyrant when she was your age," she says.

"What?" I can hardly contain my enthusiasm.

"If you can manage to stay out of a police car, you're one better than her. Now forget we had this conversation. I have cookies to bake."

I know better than to push my luck, but someday I'm going to get the rest of that story. So far my summer break is off to a great start.

Chapter 3:

The sound of a vehicle backing up—*beep, beep, beep*—at seven o'clock on a Friday morning during summer vacation when you're trying to sleep is one of the most annoying sounds I've ever heard in my twelve years of life. No amount of pillows over my head can dull the noise. I get up and look out the window. A moving van is backing into the driveway across the street from Grandma's house. The house has been empty for as long as I can remember. Grandma always said it was one day away from being knocked down. I wonder who is brave enough—or stupid enough—to buy that house.

The movers open the back of the truck and start unloading, but it's not the typical stuff you'd expect to see—no furniture, no bedding, no cardboard boxes of kitchen items or decorations. But there is lots of wood. And a table saw and a work bench and boxes of tools. I can see hammers and nail guns sitting on top of a box even from across the street looking out my bedroom window. A green minivan pulls up behind the moving truck. A man, a woman, and a boy who looks to be about my age all get out. The boy picks up some of the boxes from the back of the truck and takes them into the garage. That is where all the stuff from the truck is being unloaded.

I can hear the loud thud of metal hitting pavement as loud as if it were made on Grandma's driveway and not the neighbor's across the street. I open the window to be nosier. It's what I'm good at, after all.

"Harrison! How many times do I have to tell you to use two hands on those boxes? You have two hundred dollars to replace those tools? I don't think so. Pick them up before someone trips over them!"

The boy puts the box on the ground and picks up all the tools that he dropped. He doesn't say one word to the man I assume is his dad. The woman, who I assume is his mom, takes grocery bags into the house without saying anything. I can't believe the nerve of that guy hollering at that boy named Harrison like that. It's not like he meant to drop the tools. And the fact that he didn't sass back is amazing. I wouldn't take anyone talking to me like that—course no one in my family ever has, even when I might have deserved it.

"Dax! Pancakes are ready!" yells Grandma from downstairs. I shut the window, roll out of bed, slip on some clothes, and decide I'm starting my day with a mission. I need to rescue that boy.

Chapter 4:

I know my grandmother so well. She had pulled out brownies from the freezer and defrosted them by the time I was ready to leave the house. It's the perfect introduction I'll need to meet Harrison. I can't spend every waking minute with Grandma, and I sure don't want to give Evie and her friends too much of my awesomeness.

Everyone is inside when I cross the street in front of the once forever vacant little house. The shingles around the front windows hang crooked. I knock lightly. No one answers. I pound with my fist.

A man, the guy I heard yelling at Harrison earlier, whips the door open. "Son, if you have something to say, it better be a lot softer than that racket you were just pounding out on the door. My wife's got a splitting headache and is trying to rest."

Behind him I can see a rickety lounger chair like the kind they have at the pool in my hometown but like from thirty years ago. The woman I saw earlier is laying on the chair with one arm thrown over her forehead. "Sorry," I say at a whisper. "I wasn't sure if you could hear me with all the moving you're doing."

"What do you want, kid?" he asks. He puts his hand on his hip in irritation. I know that look well. I get it a lot from people.

"Sorry. These are for you." I don't get intimidated much, but this guy is scary. I thrust the container of Grandma's brownies into his hand. I think he softens his face muscles a little as his scowl disappears. No smile, though. "My Grandma lives in the house across the street." I point to the perfect gingerbread house with the manicured lawn that makes this house look so out of place on this street. "I'm Dax, her grandson. I'm staying for the summer."

"Thanks, kid."

"Uh, you're welcome."

Just before he closes the door, he steps outside to say one more thing. "You tell your grandma that was very kind of her. We're, uh, we're not used to people being so friendly."

"No problem," I say. I want to know where he comes from where people aren't kind, but I don't think this is the time to ask.

When he closes the door, I hear a noise in the open garage. "Hello?" I call out but not so loud as to bring scary dude back outside. I walk to the front of the garage. Through the hundreds of boxes piled up in the garage, I see the boy named Harrison unloading lightbulbs from a box. He nearly drops one on the floor when he sees me.

"Dang, you scared me," he says. "All I need is to break something else."

I laugh. "No offense, man, but I think broken things kind of fit in around here." I point toward the garbage that sits piled along the outside of the garage that's been sitting there for years, the busted garage window that's surely let in several animals over the winters, the dog claw imprints scraping the door that leads into the house.

He smiles, but you'd miss it if you weren't paying attention. He runs his hand through his shaggy blonde hair. "I'm Harrison," he says, extending his hand.

I take it and shake back. "I'm Dax. I live across the street—well, at least for the next couple of months. I'm staying with my grandmother. She's recovering from a car accident, and I'm helping out."

"That's cool," he says.

"Are you guys moving in?" I ask.

"We're going to try. As you pointed out, this place needs some work." He looks sad again.

"I'm sure the house will be great with a little bit of hard work put in," I say.

"It's going to take a lot more than hard work to fix this place up, but I don't mind. Gives me something to do. Mom says it will be good for me and Ace to bond over something."

"I just met him," I say. "Charming guy."

"Yeah, you could say that. You know when you're playing blackjack and the ace can be a value of one or an eleven depending on what your other cards are?"

I nod my head.

"Well, that's Ace all right. He can change from a one to an eleven and back again before you have time to process what just happened. One minute he's all nice and fine and the next minute he's rude and meaner than a possum protecting its young."

"Is he married to your mom?" I ask.

"Unfortunately," says Harrison.

"Sorry about that, man," I say.

"It's okay. I try to stay out of his way. I think if we had more in common, it would be better, but I pretty much stink at this house flipping stuff."

"Is that what you guys are doing with this house?" I ask. "Fixing it up to sell for more money?"

"Yeah. It's their third flip, but the first one where we're going to live onsite while we fix up the house. It's not going to be pretty. Plus, my mom's going to have a baby, so I have to do more stuff that I can't do. Ace will just yell at me more. You might want to tell your grandma to keep her windows closed."

"What if you had some help?" I ask.

"Who would help?" asks Harrison. "We don't know anyone in Bridgport."

"That's not true."

"Huh?"

"You know me."

"I just met you."

"So? I'm already bored, and the only kids I know in this town are girls that are always volunteering. I think it's time the boys of Bridgport get together and do some volunteering, too. *Dax and the Destroyers*. Yeah, I like the sound of that."

"*Dax and the Destroyers?* How is *destroying* a way to volunteer?"

"Because our first project is going to be to destroy your house. Can't flip a house without demolishing it first!"

For the first time, a smile crosses Harrison's face. He nods his head slowly in understanding. "Maybe Ace will be happy that I found a helper."

"Then that's our plan. *Dax and the Destroyers* here we come!" It's a lot cooler name than *Dax and the Defenders* anyway. Tearing stuff up is going to be awesome.

Chapter 5:

"Grandma, do you still have some of Grandpa's old tools?" I ask, as Grandma and I sit in the backyard snapping off the ends of green beans she's just picked from the garden.

"I'm positive there's still some tools in the back of the shed somewhere," she says. "When Grandpa died, your Uncle Charlie took some things that were special to him, but he left a lot. I think about cleaning that shed out every time I go in there to get the artificial Christmas tree out in December. I guess I just don't have the heart to part with things yet. Why do you ask, Dax?"

"I'm going to help the new neighbors do some house projects. They have a son—Harrison—who's about my age."

"That's nice," says Grandma. "Take whatever you like. Your Grandpa would be proud to know his only grandson takes an interest in construction."

"Kind of more like destruction first."

Grandma laughs. "You have to make a little mess before you can clean it up."

I nod like I understand. When I've finished snapping green beans, I let myself into the shed in the backyard. I have to make a path through thick cobwebs while letting my eyes adjust to the dark shadows cast in the room by a small stream of light that peaks through the dirty window of the shed. What startles me more than the cobwebs and shadows is the smell of old cigar smoke that seeps out of every wall in the small shed. It takes me back to when I was six or seven and used to hang out with Grandpa during my visits. He tried to hide his bad habit, but I know Grandma knew about his cigars. I hung onto

Grandpa's every word, sure he was the wisest man I'd ever known. I sure do miss him.

I pick through various tools that litter the top shelf of Grandpa's workbench as if he'd left them in a hurry to rush into the house when Grandma called him for dinner, though they've been sitting here for the last three years since his death. I shake off the sad memories as I pull out what I think I need—a hammer, a screwdriver, and a saw. I drop a handful of nails into an old baby food jar in case they come in handy. I'm about to leave when I see Grandpa's familiar handwriting scrawled on a scrap of paper that's been shoved into an old mayonnaise jar. I pull it out.

Make kitchen window flower box for Ma's birthday present.

The note is dated, one week before his death. I open the shed door. I can see the kitchen window on the side of the house. There is no flower box hanging outside the window. Maybe I can do something about that.

Ace is sitting on the front steps of his house when I cross the street. He waves at the tools in my hands. "We have tools, you know?" he says.

"I know. I didn't want to bug you if you were using something I needed."

"You think you know what you need?" he says.

"I think so. I used to help my Grandpa with some projects."

"Huh. You're different from Harrison."

"How so?" I say.

"He doesn't know a screwdriver from a wrench."

"Maybe he just needs someone to teach him. My dad doesn't know much about tools and projects. My mom always has to hire someone if we need something major done. If it weren't for my Grandpa teaching me a few things, she'd have to hire someone to change a lightbulb or hang a picture or mow the lawn. I'm lucky, I guess."

"Huh," Ace says again. "Harrison's dad was probably like your dad. He didn't do much with him."

"Oh, my dad does stuff with me, just not construction stuff. It's not every twelve-year-old boy who has flown a plane before! My dad taught me that. And I didn't even crash, though my mom was positive I would!"

Ace laughs. "That's something I won't be able to teach my kid."

"Maybe my dad could take Harrison up in a plane someday and give him a flying lesson."

"I don't mean Harrison, I mean my baby that's coming soon."

"Oh. I guess I think of Harrison as your kid, too— you know, since he lives with you and all."

Ace doesn't say anything for a few seconds. He nods his head as if he's agreeing with something, but I'm not sure what he's agreeing to. "Take that hammer of yours and pull out the nails holding those old shutters up. I've got new ones in the garage that need to be painted and installed. Think you could do that?"

"Sure, I can do that," I say.

"Good. I'll get Harrison to help you. Maybe you can give him a few tips."

"Okay," I say. I wonder if Ace will ever give Harrison a chance to prove he's a cool guy.

Harrison and I are removing the final shutter when I get an idea. Sometimes I amaze myself. "Flatten some of that cardboard from the new kitchen cabinet boxes. Lay it out on the grass," I say.

"Why?" he asks.

"Let's paint the new shutters."

"But Ace didn't tell us to do that."

"I know. He'll be super proud of you for taking some initiative."

"I don't know," says Harrison.

"Dude, get some confidence," I say.

"Fine." Harrison spreads cardboard onto the front lawn. He places two sets of shutters onto the cardboard. "What color?" he asks.

"What colors do you have?" I say.

He goes back into the garage. "There are cans of black spray paint and red spray paint," he says.

"Pick one."

"Pick one?" he repeats.

I roll my eyes at him.

He shakes his head. "Fine, let's paint them black," he says.

During our work, Harrison and I share stories about our friends and schools. He seems surprised, if not impressed, that I got five detentions last year. I only deserved three of them—since they all came for the same offense. I thought it was hilarious putting shaving cream on all of the classroom doors during spirit week. I mean, it wasn't easy turning the shaving cream blue and white, our school colors. The white was easy, of course, but I had to add blue food coloring to every door handle. That took work. The other detentions were complete scams. I always get blamed when someone makes some stupid noise in the class behind the teacher's back.

"I only get in trouble at home, and I'm not sure why all of the time. I was May student of the month in my middle school," he says.

"It sounds like we both need to brush off on each other to balance out." We laugh. We are almost done with the five sets of shutters when we hear the front door slam shut.

"What on earth are you doing?" It's Ace.

"We—I…I decided to paint the shutters—to surprise you. Dax is helping out."

I am so proud of Harrison.

"Your mother wanted *red* shutters…*red*. You painted them *black*."

Harrison's gaze drops to the grass next to the shutters, dotted with black paint despite trying our best not to make a mess—except for the black smiley face that I made next to the mailbox.

"I'm sorry," he says.

I glare at Ace—hoping he notices. I'm starting to think this guy shouldn't be a parent to Harrison *or* the new baby. Because even screw-ups deserve a break once in a while. Goodness knows I've been given a break or two.

Chapter 6:

"Really, Evie?" I ask. Evie and Logan and Franny are standing at my Grandma's door dressed in neon-colored shirts with *Evie and the Volunteers* written on the back. "You have to accessorize to demolish a house?" I roll my eyes.

"Dax, don't be so dramatic," says Evie.

"Yeah, Dax. It's important to wear bright colors so that we stay safe," says Franny.

"And how exactly do bright colors keep you safe?" I ask.

"Because no one is gonna swing a sledgehammer at a girl wearing neon orange," says Logan. *"Duh."* This time Logan rolls her eyes.

"Fine, whatever. Let's go. Ace was expecting us ten minutes ago. He's going to be mad."

"Mad?" says Evie. "He should be happy that we've adjusted our schedules to help with this house project. We don't exactly take on volunteer projects that involve getting dirty."

I yell *goodbye* to Grandma who is reading a magazine out on the deck. I didn't want to ask Evie and her friends to help Harrison and me, but I felt like we didn't have a choice. Ace seemed okay that I was available to help. But this project is bigger than you'd think looking at the size of the small house. Harrison says the baby is coming sooner than later, and the house needs to be ready by then. So, I caved and asked Ace if I could bring a few more people along to help take out the old kitchen cabinets. I hope he doesn't freak when he sees the color-coordinated bunch I'm bringing over.

"Boy, am I glad you're here," says Harrison.

He is standing on the driveway next to a large dumpster, throwing in pieces of wood that I can only imagine were part of the cabinets. "Sorry," I say. "I didn't know I was going to have to wait so long for the divas. I nod my head in the direction of the girls. "This is Evie, Logan, and Franny," I say, pointing to each of the girls. I've never seen such big smiles on their faces. It's disgusting.

"It's a pleasure to meet you, Harrison," says Evie.

She sticks out her hand. Harrison takes it like he's shaking a soggy lasagna noodle. I try not to laugh. "Come on," I say, putting Harrison out of his misery. I lead the way into the house through the garage door and into the kitchen. "Hi, Ace."

He grunts a *hello*. He seems startled by the girls because he sets down his sledgehammer and stares from one girl to the next for a full five seconds before speaking. "*This* is my work crew?"

Evie sticks out her hand again. *"Evie and the Volunteers* at your service, sir."

Ace actually cracks a smile. Then he shrugs his shoulders. "Well, I guess you'll do. Girls, put on those masks." He points to a portion of the countertop that remains. "No sense messing up your lungs by sucking in dirt or dust, but no guarantees you won't break a nail."

"Break a nail?" says Logan. "I haven't had nails long enough to break since I was five and my mom tried to make me wear a dress for the last time."

"Huh," says Ace. "A girl who doesn't mind a little hard work. Good. I'll swing the sledgehammer. You kids haul the cabinets and countertops to the dumpster. Watch for nails."

Harrison, Evie, Logan, Franny, and I take as much debris as we can carry out to the dumpster, sometimes carrying individual loads, sometimes helping each other with big pieces.

"What's that guy's problem with girls?" asks Franny after a few loads. She hasn't said much at all today.

"He doesn't have anything against girls," says Harrison. "He just doesn't like people in general.

"Why?" asks Evie.

"His parents died when he was young. He had to raise his little brother on his own. Mom says he feels like everyone in his life lets him down."

"Well, maybe if he didn't expect everyone to let him down, they wouldn't," says Franny.

"What do you mean?" asks Logan.

"If you expect bad stuff to happen, then you look for bad stuff to happen. You miss all the good stuff in between the bad stuff. Sounds like Ace is looking for people to let him down and missing when people help him out."

"Like us," I say. "Now quit jabbering and get back to helping out." Logan brushes past me, knocking me into the side of the dumpster. It takes everything I have not to give her a shove back.

Harrison's mom Jill has a pitcher with lemonade and ice sitting on a coffee table in the front room when we return to the house. "Take a break kids." She hands us each a glass to drink.

"Thanks," we all say in unison.

"Ace and I can't thank you enough for all of your help. This project would take three times as long if we didn't have your help. And goodness knows, we don't have much time left before the baby comes." She pats her growing belly.

"Make sure you drink some of that lemonade, too." Ace speaks from the kitchen, but it's such a small house it sounds like he's right next to us.

Jill smiles. "He is so caring," she says.

We all nod like we agree, but I am positive that most of the rest of us in the room have yet to see that side of Ace. I'm glad she does, though.

"*What was that?*" Evie is screaming and pointing to the corner of the room.

Her screaming brings Ace into the room immediately. He follows Evie's finger into the corner of the room. That's when I see it, too. A long tail slides behind the cracks in the drywall. It's not just any tail, either. It's the tail of a large four-legged rodent. And where there is one, there are usually many. Rats in the walls—not any new homeowner's dream pet, especially a homeowner living in a construction site with a new baby on the way.

"Oh no!" says Jill.

"It's okay. I'll call the exterminator. Just have to lay low for a couple of days," says Ace, patting Jill's arm.

"No!" she screams again.

Rats sure bring a strong reaction. Can't say I blame her, though.

"*No!*" Jill screams again. "It's not…the rat. I…I think the baby is coming."

Chapter 7:

"I can't find the ladder!" yells Evie from the open front door.

"It's behind the shed in the backyard," I yell back, "but you shouldn't be using the ladder alone. Wait for me."

"I'm quite capable of putting up those shutters, thank you very much," she says, "Plus, Franny and Logan are helping."

The door slams shut. I roll my eyes. Those girls drive me nuts. But, truth is, I am so grateful they are here. I just won't tell them how much their help is needed. Ever since Jill and Ace took off for the hospital yesterday afternoon, we've been crazy busy, spending every waking minute here, except for sleeping hours. Ace talked to Grandma and agreed to allow Harrison stay over at her house until they are home from the hospital. The baby isn't born yet. Since it's a few weeks early, the doctors are trying to delay the birth a little longer so the baby can get stronger, or something like that. Thinking about babies and the whole birth thing makes me feel like puking, so I don't think about it any longer than I have to. Plus, it's good that the baby's not born yet. It gives us more time to work here. The way the house looks right now, Harrison's family will have to go to a hotel. I imagine that's the last thing the family wants.

The girls came over yesterday evening. They've taken on the shutters project. They are repainting the shutters red like Jill wanted although it took a long argument to talk Logan out of alternating red and black shutters. Now they are hanging them. Can't guarantee they'll be straight, but they'll be up. Harrison and I took all the trash and demolished materials out of the house.

The doorbell rings, kind of sounding like a sick cat. That will have to be a project for later down the road.

"Come in," I hear Harrison say. "Thanks for coming. We saw the rat in this wall over here," he says. He walks to the corner of the room.

"Hey," I say. I wave at the guy wearing the *You don't want'm. We'll handle'm* t-shirt. Thank goodness Grandma knows a lot of people who love her. She called one of her most loyal library patrons and asked for a favor. He sent over what he called his best guy to handle the rat extermination. Ace doesn't even know yet. It was Harrison's idea to see if I might know anyone who could do it. I wish Ace knew how he was stepping up to the plate for his family.

The exterminator, a guy named Vince according to his nametag, starts poking at the wall with a stick. "Hmm, sounds hollow right here. I'm gonna go outside and take a look."

Harrison and I look at each other. "I think we should make a list of what we can do before my family gets back," says Harrison. "I know we can't put in the new kitchen cabinets, but we can give this place a good cleaning, paint the baby's room and maybe the living room. Mom purchased the paint. I saw it in the garage. I wish we could get some furniture or decorations to make the house look a little prettier."

"How about the thrift store a few blocks away?" says a quiet voice.

We both turn around, startled. It's Franny. We didn't hear her open the door. "What do you know about it?" I ask.

"I know that a lot of people who go to the food pantry where we volunteer will also go there. Your Grandma knows about it. I've heard her send people there before who were looking for household items."

"That might be a good idea," I say. "If we pool our money, maybe we can…"

"*Run!*"

"Huh?" says Harrison. "I don't think we have to run. The stuff's not going anywhere."

"*No, I mean run! There's a rat!*" screams Franny.

Franny jumps onto the only chair in the room, a rickety lawn chair that Jill has been using as a kind of recliner. But as she stands on it, the bottom weaving breaks apart, leaving her feet stuck in the middle and back on the floor again. She drags the chair across the floor and falls forward, landing in Harrison's arms. The look of terror on her face sends me into a fit of laughter.

The front door bursts open. Evie and Logan run in to see the source of the commotion, but all they see is their scaredy-cat friend in the arms of my new friend. I hold my side from laughing so hard. "I don't know if you're more scared of that rat or of being in Harrison's dirty grip!"

"What's going on?" says Logan. Her hands are on her hips and her finger is wagging at me like I've done something wrong.

"Yeah!" says Evie. "What did you do to Franny?"

Harrison unglues Franny's death grip from his shirt and helps her get out of the chair. In the meantime, the rat's not quite done with his visit. Likely he's more terrified of us than Franny is of him. He scurries out from his hiding place behind a toolbox in the kitchen, nearly running over Evie's foot. She screams and steps backwards, tripping over a loose rug. She drops the can of red paint she is holding.

"Not the floor!" I yell. I grab a roll of paper towels and try to stop the stream of red paint from soaking in to the floor.

"There's still a rat in here!" yells Franny.

She points to the corner of the room. The rat is moving slowly now. Maybe he thinks we can't see him if he moves like that. Maybe they're not as crafty as everyone thinks they are. Then in one leap, he dives back into the hole in the wall. A loud commotion carries through the wall that involves some choice words. Then *silence*.

A few minutes later, Vince the exterminator walks through the front door. "I handled'm," he says. A giant grin spreads across his face.

"What does that mean?" asks Franny who is now standing on the only remaining kitchen cabinet.

"Rat's in a cage in the back of my truck."

"Aren't there more?" I ask.

"Don't think so. I tapped around the walls, took a peek in the hole. There's a pile of bricks on the other side of the wall. One or two of them must have gotten tossed in that pile a little too hard, made a hole all the way through the drywall. That's how that rat got in, but the drywall is strong all around that hole. Mr. Rat was just going in and out, not making a nest or anything like that."

"That's a relief," says Harrison. "Thanks." He pulls out a plastic baggie from his back pocket and takes out a twenty-dollar bill to give to Vince.

"No, kid. This one's on me—not a big job at all. And from the sound of it, you guys on this side of the wall had a little fun, too." He smiles at Franny before walking back out the door.

"I wonder how those bricks pierced the side of the house," says Harrison.

"Hmm," I say. Perhaps this is not a good time to tell him that I was using the new patio bricks to practice my super fantastic fastball pitch when I *stacked* them by the house. That conversation can wait.

Chapter 8:

"Babies need stimulation," says Evie like she knows anything about babies. She's the youngest kid in her family.

"Babies need diapers and food. They don't need anything else," I say.

"No, she's right," says Harrison.

Whose side is he on?

"I watched a show with Mom about how babies learn to track stuff with their eyes. They make these special mobiles."

"What in the world is a *mobile*?" I ask.

"Seriously, Dax?" says Logan.

"A mobile is like a toy that hangs over the baby's crib that turns around or plays music. The baby likes to watch it and listen to it," says Franny.

It was not my idea to bring the girls shopping at the thrift store. Their know-it-all attitudes are getting old. But when they pulled out a hundred dollars that they'd raised at a lemonade stand and donated it all to Harrison's family, it was hard to tell them they couldn't come shopping with us. "Fine, you stick to the baby's room stuff. We will buy for the house. Is that okay with you, Harrison?"

"Yeah, that's fine, but I will need some girl opinions. I, uh, I want to make sure my mom likes the stuff I pick out."

"I'll help you, Harrison," says Franny.

Geesh. She falls into his arms running away from a rat and now she's his right-hand girl. "Well, let's quit talking and start shopping. I bet we don't have much time before they come home," I say.

Evie and Logan head toward the back room of the thrift shop where the kids' stuff is kept. Harrison, Franny, and I start looking through the rows and rows of household items. I concentrate on kitchen stuff like pots and pans because Harrison says they don't have a whole lot while he and Franny look for decorations like lamps and throw rugs.

"I like this rug better," says Franny. "It has a nice, colorful geometric pattern. It's soft and will really brighten up the living room."

"I like it," says Harrison. "I think that gray lamp will look nice in the room, too, since there's gray in the background of the rug."

"Oh, definitely," says Franny.

It's like they have their own design show on HGTV. It makes me want to puke. "Shouldn't you be looking for furniture first before picking accent pieces?" I say. Oh man. Who am I sounding like now? I've been watching too much television with Grandma.

"Excellent point, Dax," says Franny.

"Furniture costs a lot of money," says Harrison, "even used furniture."

"True," says Franny, "but let's see if we can pick out a nice chair, at least for your mom to sit in with the baby."

By the time we are ready to leave, we have filled three shopping carts plus found a gray glider chair and a side table that won't fit in a cart. Harrison pulls out his plastic baggie with all the money collected from everyone. He crosses his fingers. I'm guessing he's hoping he has enough money and doesn't have to put some things back.

The sales clerk gives Harrison an odd look, kind of judgmental. I guess I can't blame her as it's not every day that a bunch of eleven and twelve-year-olds buy $214.23 worth of household and baby stuff. Luckily Harrison has enough money. Grandma chipped in a little money, too. Plus, she said we could have the old loveseat couch from the basement since no one goes down there much anymore since Grandpa died. That's where he had his amateur radio collection. Every time I came to visit, he and I would try to contact other amateur radio guys, or *ham radio operators*, as they are called. We used a special code called the Morse code. I still remember how to spell my name using the code. Dah dit dit, dit dah, dah dit dit dah. Man, I miss those days.

I take the fullest cart because I'm the strongest, after all. But when Logan sails past me with her cart, my competitive spirit takes over. I run with all my might and jump on the back of the cart, coasting past Logan…and into another cart that hangs outside of the cart return in the parking lot. The new *old* lamp goes flying off the cart. I never saw Harrison coming in from behind, until I see his body doing a somersault on the hard cement. But he's victorious, coming up with the lamp in his hand—safe and secure. His knee on the other hand has seen better days.

"Dax, look what you've done!" yells Evie. "Is that why you call yourselves *Dax and the Destroyers*?"

"*Not funny, Evie!* And it wasn't even my fault. That little volunteer of yours challenged me to a race. What was I supposed to do?" I say.

"I didn't challenge you to anything," says Logan. "I was just stretching my legs, and you couldn't stand a girl passing you up!"

"Guys!"

We both stop and stare at Franny who almost never yells. "We need to get Harrison home. He's bleeding and needs to be cleaned up!"

She is kneeling on the ground next to Harrison who is using a tissue from Franny's purse to stop the bleeding. We hang our heads in agreement and push the carts all the way back to Harrison's house. For some reason, I get the

job of pushing the carts all the way back *by myself*..
Sometimes life isn't fair.

Chapter 9:

The paint is dry in the living room and the baby's room. With the gray, yellow, and white throw rug in the center of the living room and the glider rocker and Grandma's loveseat positioned with the end table between them, this is starting to look like a real room. It was a huge help that the guy in line behind us at the thrift store volunteered to drop off the heavy furniture. Evie sets the lamp on the end table and plugs it in. Franny sets a vase on the coffee table that the family already owned. She puts yellow flowers from her yard inside the vase. Logan grabs a hammer and nail before I can stop her. She hangs a picture frame we bought at the thrift store. In the frame is a picture of Ace, Jill, and a younger Harrison.

"Where'd you find that?" asks Harrison, standing up from the loveseat so quickly he almost knocks over the vase.

"I found it in the bedroom. There's a whole box of pictures," says Logan.

"You don't like it?" asks Franny, softly.

"It's…it's okay," says Harrison, "as long as Ace isn't mad at me for doing all this." He points around the room which looks completely different from the disaster his family left two days ago. It really is a miraculous makeover.

"Why would he be mad?" asks Evie. "He will love it, Harrison."

"I hope so," he says.

"Have some confidence, man," I say. "You've done a good thing here." I slap him on the back, trying to wipe the frown from his face.

"Okay," he says. "You're right."

"Come see the baby's room," says Evie. "It looks amazing."

We are about to see the girls' transformation of the baby's room when the front door opens. In walks Grandma. She has a huge smile on her face. "Hi, kids. Wow! This place looks great. I am so proud of you."

"What's up, Grandma?" I say.

She turns toward Harrison. "I have some wonderful news! Ace just called to check on you. He also wanted me to tell you that your mom had her baby!"

"She did?" he asks, sinking back into the loveseat. "Is…is she okay?"

"She's great," says Grandma.

"And the baby?" he says.

"The baby is perfect, too. She has all of her toes and fingers and is even bigger than they thought she'd be since she was born a few weeks early."

"*She?*"

"Yes, *she*, Harrison. You have a little sister."

"That's the best news in the world," says Evie. "She can be our first volunteer-in-training."

"No way," I say. "There's no reason why she can't be a *destroyer-in-training*."

"Maybe we should let her decide," says Franny, ever the voice of reason.

Logan and I each throw a couch pillow at her. Harrison comes to her defense, though. "Franny is right. Did Ace say when they are coming home?"

"Probably tomorrow, but Ace is coming over soon to pick you up to see the baby in the hospital."

"What? The house isn't ready yet!" Harrison looks panicked. "We wanted to clean up the bathroom and mow the yard."

"I have a little shopping to do. I could drop you off at the hospital," says Grandma, "if that would help."

"Thanks! That would be great. Can you call him now? And can Dax come, too—uh, for support or whatever," he says, looking at the ground.

"Meet me in my garage in ten minutes."

"Don't worry about a thing," says Evie, taking charge. "We will transform that bathroom—scrub the tiles, hang up the shower curtain…"

"Fill the soap dispenser…" says Logan.

"Clean the mirror…" says Franny.

"And Logan's got the toilet covered," says Evie.

"Hey! Why do I get the toilet?" she asks.

"Thanks, girls! See you later! You can use the extra money to order a pizza if your parents don't care," says Harrison.

Harrison stands outside the hospital room for a long time. I finally have to push him toward the door.

"What are you afraid of?" I say.

"I'm not afraid."

"Yes, you are."

"No, *I'm not.*" He turns the knob of the door to his mom's room. I follow him but stand back. Babies still make me nervous. Plus, this should be a private reunion.

"Harrison!" says his mom. "Come here and meet your baby sister."

I hear a lot of baby noises, but they're not coming from the baby. They're coming from Harrison making goofy sounds at the baby. It's kind of embarrassing, but I've never had a baby in my family, so maybe it's normal.

"She's kind of cute, isn't she?" asks Ace.

I see Harrison shake his head in agreement.

"What should we name her?" asks Jill.

"She doesn't have a name?" says Harrison.

"Not yet," she says. "We are still narrowing down our list. She came a little sooner than we thought she would. We just can't agree."

"Want to help us?" says Ace.

"Are you serious?" he says.

"Ace and I are very proud of you," says Jill.

Did someone tell them what we've been doing at the house? I wonder.

"Yeah, you haven't caused too much damage yet," says Ace.

"*Ace!*" says Jill.

"Just kidding, Harrison. You made friends quickly and got them to help take out those cabinets and do some demolition work. That was helpful. The house is going to be a disaster when we get home, but at least a lot of the removal of the old stuff is done. Yes, that's a big help."

"You're welcome," says Harrison.

"So, want to know our name choices?" asks Jill.

"Sure," he says.

I decide to step out of the hall. It's really none of my business being here. Harrison doesn't need my support. He can stand on his own now. He's a big brother after all. And maybe having a baby has softened Ace up a little. It's a win-win situation.

Chapter 10:

Harrison is finishing mowing the lawn, and I am sweeping the grass off the driveway when Ace pulls up to the curb in the green minivan. Harrison and I look at each other, not sure how he's going to react. He doesn't seem to focus on anything but getting the car door unstuck so that he can get Jill and the baby out. I guess there's more than just their house that needs some help.

"What happened?" says Jill.

"I don't know," says Ace. He sets the baby carrier down.

"Did you pay someone to paint those shutters?" she asks. "Because they look beautiful."

"No, I haven't been to the house since you went into labor earlier in the week. Harrison has been staying at the neighb…"

Then he sees Harrison and me. "Harrison?"

"Y…yes?"

"Did you do this?" He points to the yard and the shutters and even the cleaned-up garage.

I can tell that Harrison is considering whether to answer truthfully. "Yes…well…no…I mean—I did a lot of this stuff. Dax helped." He points to me. "And those girls, *Evie and the Volunteers.*"

"The ones with those goofy-colored shirts?"

Harrison laughs. "Yes, those girls."

"Why? Why'd you do all this?"

"I wanted to help…the family."

"It looks great," says Jill.

"Thanks," says Harrison.

The baby starts crying which returns everyone to the moment. Ace picks up the baby carrier with one hand and with his other hand gently guides his wife to the door. I hope new mothers don't have bad hearts or anything like that because if she was surprised by the outside of the house, I can't imagine what she'll do when she sees the inside.

"Dax, thanks for your help," says Ace. "Do you think your Grandma will mind if Harrison stays with you a few more nights? I have to get an exterminator out here to take care of that rat problem before we can stay in the house. Jill wanted to get a few of the baby's things she has in the garage before we go to a hotel."

"Uh…sure," I say. I put my hand over my mouth so I don't laugh out loud.

Jill opens the door first. She is followed into the house by Ace who is still holding the baby carrier. Then Harrison and I enter. Usually screaming means that something bad has happened but not this time. And it's not coming from the baby, either. Jill grabs hold of Ace's arm for support. I'm still wondering how strong new mom's hearts are, but I think I'm just making stuff up in my mind.

"Harrison—Harrison, did you and your friends…do all of this, too?" she asks. Her eyes are moving around the room—the loveseat, the glider, the lamp, the end table, the pillows, the colorful rug, the flowers.

Ace is staring at the wall that used to give that rat entry into the house. Harrison notices.

"Dax's Grandma knew an exterminator. He got the rat. There was only one. There was a hole in only one spot in the drywall that it came in and out of. There aren't any nests. We piled the bricks up on the outside wall extra tight to make sure nothing else gets in, but you have to fix the drywall. I don't know how to do that," he says.

"Harrison, this is simply amazing," says Ace. "I didn't give you any credit. I'm…I'm sorry."

I look at Jill. She is crying. She nudges Ace toward Harrison. He reaches out his arms. It's not the most natural looking invitation for a hug, but it's all that Harrison needs to lean in to receive it. I am beginning to think I should have waited outside.

The doorbell rings. The baby starts crying. Jill takes her out of the carrier. Ace answers the door.

"Hi, Ace."

Ugh. It's *Evie and the Volunteers*. They just can't stay away.

"Hello, girls," says Jill. "Please come in. We want to thank you for everything you've done to help our family."

"It was our pleasure," says Logan.

"We brought you dinner, too," says Franny. "I know that Harrison likes meatloaf."

How did she find that out?

"And since your kitchen is still torn apart, my mom had us come right over as soon as the meatloaf was done, so it would still be warm," says Evie. "I'll set it on the counter—or what's left of the counter."

The baby starts crying again but not hard, more with a little whimper. That sets the girls off with a bunch of *oohing and ahhing* about how cute the baby is. It's gross.

"What's the baby's name?" asks Logan.

"Why don't you tell her, Harrison?" says Jill. "He got to make the final decision." She smiles at her son and for just a second it makes me miss my own mother. But it also reminds me to ask Grandma again why mom rode in a police car once when she was younger.

"Addison Elizabeth," says Harrison. His face turns the color of the tomatoes in Grandma's garden.

"I think it's perfect," says Franny. "*Harrison* and *Addison*."

"Enough cuteness," I say. "Maybe the baby should go to bed now."

"Dax!" says Evie. "That's so rude!"

I look at Evie with bug eyes. Girls can be clueless sometimes. Doesn't she get that I'm trying to get Harrison's parents to finish their house tour? "I just *meant* that the baby might need some *stimulation with her mobile.*"

Then the lightbulb turns on in her head. "Ohhhhh," says Evie. "Yeah, that's a good idea."

Harrison shakes his head from Evie to me and back again. "Come see Addison's room," he says.

Yeah, maybe that would have been an easier tactic. Everyone goes into the room except for Evie and me. No sense making the room seem even tinier than it already is.

"You did a good thing here, Dax," says Evie though she says it so quietly I can barely make out what she is saying.

"I was just trying to find something to do that didn't involve spending all of my summer with *Evie and the Volunteers.*"

"How's that working out for you?" she says.

"I didn't realize that asking you guys to help *one* day meant that I wasn't going to get rid of you."

Evie smiles. "I know you love us, Dax. You can't help it."

I pick up one of the throw pillows and wing it at her head. Too bad she's got quick reflexes and catches it mid-air, returning it to its proper place on the loveseat just as the renovation tour group returns to the living room.

"So, Ace," I say. "Think you are going to make a good profit on this house flip when you sell it?"

Jill looks at Ace and nods her head. "Well, Dax. It seems that we've had a change of heart."

"What do you mean?" asks Logan.

"We aren't selling this house flip," says Ace.

"We're not?" asks Harrison.

"We're not," repeats Ace. "I think we may have finally found a community of people that have welcomed us, at least a group of friends for you, Harrison, that have welcomed you. That's important to your mom—and me."

I am *not* the crying kind, but I can tell Harrison is having a hard time not letting a few tears fall down his face. But he recovers nicely. "That's cool," he says.

I need to get out of mushville. "I need to get going. I have a few things to do for Grandma."

Ace reaches out his hand for me to shake. "Thanks again, Dax, for all of your help. We've got a lot more projects around here if you're bored."

"Sure, I'd like to help. Someone has to keep Harrison out of trouble." I laugh.

Ace looks at Harrison. "I think he's a lot more capable than I ever knew."

Chapter 11:

Grandma gets home late from the library. She returned to her job as the director, but she only works three days a week. She moves a little bit slower than she did before the car accident in the winter.

"I'm in the backyard!" I yell when I hear her calling my name from inside the house.

"There you are. I thought maybe you were across the street."

"No, I need a break. Anyway, that baby makes a lot of noise. Plus, did you know baby's poop like twenty times a day?"

Grandma laughs. "No, I didn't know it was twenty times a day, but I suppose it is quite a lot. You were the same way, too, you know?"

"Grandma, cut it out! That's disgusting! Come here. I want to show you something." I start walking to the side of the house, the side where the kitchen window faces Grandma's rose garden.

"Dax, did you clip the gutter again when you were mowing?"

"No, Grandma. It's nothing like that."

Grandma stops moving the minute she sees it—a flower box underneath her kitchen window.

"I know you were supposed to have one of those a few years ago when Grandpa was alive. I found a note he'd written in his shed reminding him to make one for you. I guess he got sick before he could. I didn't know if you wanted anything special. I hope it's okay that I used some of the scraps of wood from the neighbors' old kitchen cabinets to make what I thought a flower box was supposed to look like. I bought some clearance flowers at the grocery store, so I'm not sure how long they will live."

"Dax, stop talking." She puts her hand on my arm. "I love it. It's perfect. Making me a kitchen flower box was the only promise your Grandpa never kept to me." A tear falls onto her cheek.

"Well, I guess he kept his promise after all. I never would have made it if I hadn't seen his note."

"You're a special kid, Dax." Grandma grabs my head and pulls me in for a hug.

"There is something in the air around this town lately. I need to find some trouble soon because I'm going to lose my reputation of being a tough kid."

"Just like your mother, aren't you?"

"If you say so. Maybe this would be a good time to tell me about that little ride she took in a police car."

Grandma laughs. "Let's just say it involved a chicken coop at the mayor's house, a can of paint, too much time, and a lot of creativity."

Now I know for a fact that it's my mom's fault when I don't follow all of life's rules. It's in my blood. That's my defense, and I'm sticking to it.

Please consider leaving a review. Thank you.

Dax and the Destroyers, Book 2, Park Restoration is available now.

Evie and the Volunteers Series

    Join ten-year-old Evie and her friends as they volunteer all over town meeting lots of cool people and getting into just a little bit of trouble. There is no place left untouched by their presence, and what they get from the people they meet is greater than any amount of money.

    Book 1   Animal Shelter

    Book 2   Nursing Home

    Book 3   After-School Program

    Book 4   Food Pantry

    Book 5: Public Library

Other Children's Books by Marcy Blesy:

Confessions of a Corn Kid:

Twelve-year-old Bernie Taylor doesn't fit in. She wants to be an actress but not your typical country-music lovin', beef-eatin' actress you'd expect from Cornville, Illinois. No way. She wants to go to Chicago to be a real actress, just like her mom did before she died of breast cancer. Bernie keeps a journal that her Mom gave her and writes down all her confessions, the deepest feelings of her heart, 'cause she doesn't want any of those regrets Mom talked about. Regrets sound too much like those bubbly blisters she keeps getting on her feet from trying to fit into last year's designer knock-off shoes. But it's not easy for Bernie to pursue her dreams. Her dad just doesn't understand. Plus, she's tired of being bullied for being different. Why can't middle schoolers wear runway fashions to school?

Then, during the announcement of the sixth grade play, Bernie's teacher reveals that there will be one scholarship to a prestigious performing arts camp in Chicago. Bernie knows it's her one big chance to achieve her dream. She spends too much time dreaming of the lead role in the play (which includes kissing Cameron Edmunds) and not enough time practicing her audition lines. She bumbles her lines, blows her audition, and battles her bully, Dixie Moxley, reigning Jr. Miss Corn Harvest Queen. She digs in with the heels of her hand-me-down knee-high boots, determined to win that scholarship-somehow. If she doesn't, she'll be stuck in Cornville forever, far away from the spotlight she craves.

Am I Like My Daddy? :

Join seven-year-old Grace on her journey through coping with the loss of her father while learning about the different ways that people grieve the loss of a loved one. In the process of learning about who her father was through the eyes of others, she learns about who she is today because of her father's personality and love. *Am I Like My Daddy?* is a book designed to help children who are coping with the loss of a loved one. Children are encouraged to express through journaling what may be so difficult to express through everyday conversation. *Am I Like My Daddy?* teaches about loss through reflection.

Am I Like My Daddy? is an important book in the children's grief genre. Many books in this genre deal with the time immediately after a loved one dies. This book focuses on years after the death, when a maturing child is reprocessing his or her grief. New questions arise in the child's need to fill in those memory gaps.

Be the Vet:

Do you like dogs and cats?

Have you ever thought about being a veterinarian?

Place yourself as the narrator in seven unique stories about dogs and cats. When a medical emergency or illness impacts the pet, you will have the opportunity to diagnose the problem and suggest treatment. Following each story is the treatment plan offered by Dr. Ed Blesy, a 20 year practicing veterinarian. You will learn veterinary terms and diagnoses while being entertained with fun, interesting stories.

This is the first book in the BE THE VET series.

For ages 9-12

Be the Vet, Volume 2: November 2016

Made in the USA
Middletown, DE
28 May 2020